Brushtail
the rock wallaby

Written by Diana Petersen
Illustrated by Rich Richardson

D1263088

GOLDEN PRESS

First published 1975
Reprinted 1984
by Golden Press Pty. Ltd.
Incorporated in N.S.W.
5-01 Henry Lawson Business Centre,
Birkenhead Point, Drummoyne, N.S.W. 2047, Australia
and 717 Rosebank Road, Avondale,
Auckland, New Zealand

© 1975 Golden Press Pty. Ltd.

ISBN 0 85558 218 9

Printed in Singapore
by Tien Mah Litho Printing Company

Happily Brushtail nibbled at the green leaf he held in his paws. Down below the road was still wet from the heavy rain that had fallen all week. Now the clouds had blown away and the early morning sun shone on the ledge where the little rock wallaby sat.

Around him the other rock wallabies nibbled at the grass or sunned themselves on the warm rocks.

And at the end of the road where it came to a farm in the valley, someone else was very happy to see the sun shining.

'Hurray!' shouted Timmy. 'It's stopped raining at last! Now we can go to town today! Will we have lunch with Grandma when we've finished shopping?'

'Yes,' smiled his father.

'And can we stop to watch if we see any rock wallabies on the way?' he begged.

'Don't we always?' laughed Dad.

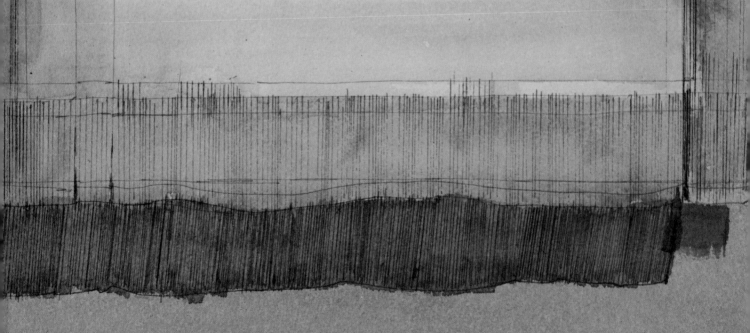

'There they are!' called Timmy as Dad's utility slowed on the bend. When the wallabies heard the utility they were off. They bounded away up the side of the mountain with their tails curved upward and their paws held in close to their chests.

'Don't they ever fall?' asked Timmy as he watched the sturdy little animals springing from rock to rock, up the almost sheer sides of the cliff.

'They have special rough pads on the soles of their feet to stop them slipping, and their thick, bushy tails help them keep their balance,' explained Dad.

He stopped the utility and he and Timmy climbed up on to a nearby rock.

'If we stay quite still they might come back,' Dad whispered.

In a few seconds the wallabies stopped and looked down at the people below. They sat stiff and alert, their heads all turned the same way—except Brushtail. He was busily pulling at a juicy fern shoot and took no notice of them at all.

'Look at that one! He's only a little one, isn't he Dad?'

Hearing Timmy's whisper, Brushtail turned. His big, brown eyes were quite still but his soft, black nose quivered. He held his ears stiffly, then twisted one ear right round to the side, listening for the strange sound which had disturbed him.

Timmy hardly dared to breathe. Suddenly Brushtail turned and sprang away, up across the jagged rocks, back to his mother.

'Come on. We'll see them on the way back,' promised Dad. 'They always come out again in the late afternoon to feed.'

'I hope I see that baby one again,' sighed Timmy. 'I wish he hadn't gone jumping away like that.'

After the utility had driven off the wallabies came back to their favourite rocks, leaping along paths polished as shiny as glass by the feet of rock wallabies. Countless generations had been using these same tracks for thousands of years.

Brushtail played happily with the other young wallabies until the sun rose higher and he began to feel sleepy.

He hopped down the slope to where his mother dozed at the mouth of a cave. Pushing past her Brushtail stretched out in the coolness at the back of the cave and was soon fast asleep.

The day wore on. Except for the buzzing of the bees, everything was quiet. Then out of the afternoon silence a stone rattled down the slope—first one stone, and then another.

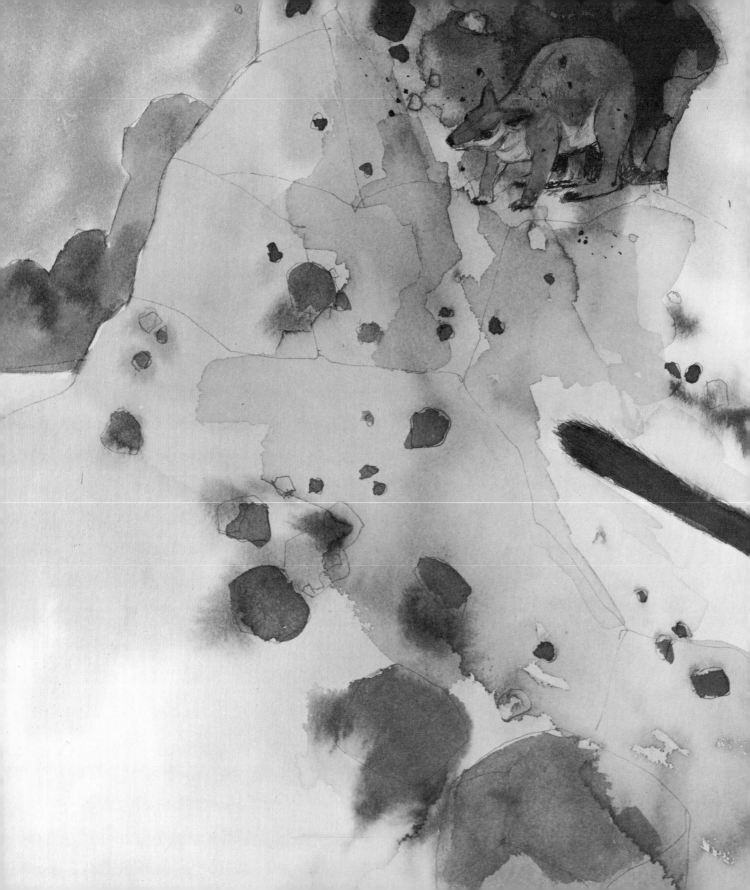

Brushtail's mother started to her feet as the first pebbles and stones clattered on to the ledge. She gave a warning 'Thump! Thump!' with her hind foot. Even as she did this a great shower of stone and rock came thundering down the side of the mountain.

With a mighty leap she was off the ledge—streaking after the other wallabies.

The heavy rain had loosened the earth above the road, and now, with a roar, it came crashing down.

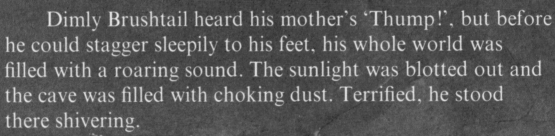

Dimly Brushtail heard his mother's 'Thump!', but before
he could stagger sleepily to his feet, his whole world was
filled with a roaring sound. The sunlight was blotted out and
the cave was filled with choking dust. Terrified, he stood
there shivering.

When at last the dust had cleared, only a small crack of
sunlight slanted into the cave.

Brushtail was trapped!

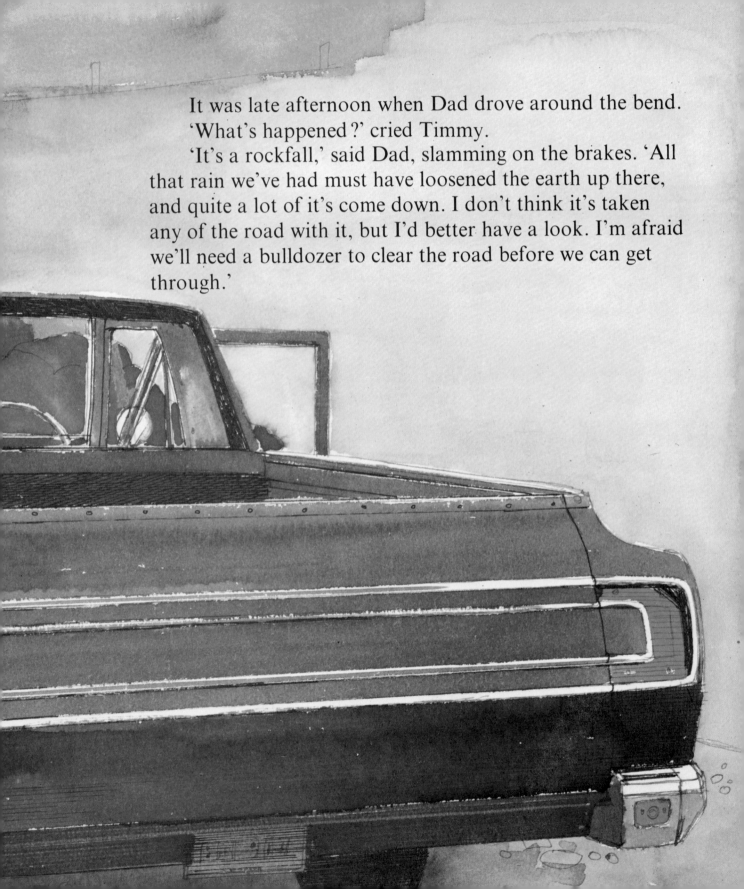

It was late afternoon when Dad drove around the bend.
'What's happened?' cried Timmy.

'It's a rockfall,' said Dad, slamming on the brakes. 'All
that rain we've had must have loosened the earth up there,
and quite a lot of it's come down. I don't think it's taken
any of the road with it, but I'd better have a look. I'm afraid
we'll need a bulldozer to clear the road before we can get
through.'

While his father examined the road, Timmy watched one of the wallabies. She was standing at the side of the slide, and although Timmy climbed towards her she didn't move.

'Tim!' called Dad sharply. 'Don't go near that fallen rock! It's dangerous!'

But Timmy was still watching the wallaby.

'Look at her Dad,' he called. 'She's frightened of me, but she hasn't run away like the others. I think something's wrong.'

As Dad began to scramble up the slope he heard a scrabbling sound.

'Shhh! Tim, did you hear that?'

'It's coming from that crack there,' said Timmy excitedly. 'What do you think it is?'

'I'll get the spade from the utility and we'll see,' said his father.

Carefully he worked the spade into the crevice, scraping the loose dirt and stones from under the ledge. It took some time, but at last he managed to widen the crack a little. He bent down to peer in.

At first nothing happened—then a little black nose and two bright eyes appeared. There was a great deal of scratching and scrabbling, then out squeezed Brushtail, sending a fresh shower of stones rattling down the slope.

Dazzled by the slanting rays of the setting sun, he stood quite still for several seconds. Then he turned, leaping away after his mother, up to the caves at the top of the mountain.

'There, he's safe now,' smiled Dad. 'Come on. We'll go back to town for the night. The bulldozer will come out in the morning and clear the road.'

'Perhaps I'll see him again when we come back tomorrow,' said Timmy, following his father back to the utility.

High above the road Brushtail watched until the utility had disappeared round the bend. Then he hopped across to his mother and began to nibble at the green grass.